This book was donated by

the Hummel Family

in honor of

the Kids

November 1994

May'naise Sandwiches & Sunshine Tea

story by SANDRA BELTON

illustrations by GAIL GORDON CARTER

FOUR WINDS PRESS ✾ New York

MAXWELL MACMILLAN CANADA   Toronto

MAXWELL MACMILLAN INTERNATIONAL   New York Oxford Singapore Sydney

Four Winds Press
Macmillan Publishing Company
866 Third Avenue
New York, NY 10022

Maxwell Macmillan Canada, Inc.
1200 Eglinton Avenue East
Suite 200
Don Mills, Ontario M3C 3N1

Macmillan Publishing Company is part of the
Maxwell Communication Group of Companies.

FIRST EDITION

Printed in Hong Kong by South China Printing Company (1988) Ltd.
on chlorine-free, acid-free paper
10 9 8 7 6 5 4 3 2 1
The text of this book is set in Centaur.
The illustrations are rendered in watercolor and pencil.
Book design by Christy Hale
Library of Congress Cataloging-in-Publication Data
Belton, Sandra.
May'naise sandwiches & sunshine tea / story by Sandra Belton ;
illustrations by Gail Gordon Carter. — 1st ed.
p.   cm.
Summary: Big Mama reminisces with her grandchild
about a childhood experience that helped inspire her to be
the first member of her family to attend college.
ISBN 0-02-709035-3
[1. Grandmothers—Fiction. 2. Afro-Americans—Fiction.]
I. Carter, Gail Gordon, ill. II. Title. III. Title: Mayonnaise sandwiches and sunshine tea.
PZ7.B4197May   1994
[E]—dc20   93-46781

To my son, Allen Douglass, who, like the first A.D.,
will always be able to see that old sun dance!

—S.B.

To my daughter, Claire Elyse

—G.G.C.

See that book on the shelf over there? That's Big Mama's scrapbook. She calls it her book of rememberies.

I don't bother Big Mama's book when she's not around. She told me not to. "This book is already raggedy enough," she says.

Anyhow, it's more fun to look through the book with Big Mama. She talks about things I wouldn't notice just looking at the pictures and other stuff by myself.

Like why Uncle Jackson had his picture taken with a hat on. Big Mama said he was proud of being in the army and wanted everybody to look at his picture and know right away he was a soldier.

Like how Keith and Kenneth were special because they were the only set of twins in the family. Nobody ever took a picture of one without the other. Even when they were almost grown.

Like how much I look like Greatgrand Hallie. How we have the same eyes.

Big Mama keeps the old flowers and handkerchiefs she has in her book wrapped in plastic. "This old stuff would probably turn to dust if the air hit it," she says.

I love it when Big Mama and I stretch out together on her bed and look through her book. We do it a lot. Especially on days when it's raining and I can't play outside with Francine and Puddin'.

The best parts of Big Mama's book are the pages that have a bunch of pictures crowded together. Big Mama calls these pages her wraparounds. "There's a story wrapped around these pictures," she says.

I can tell that Big Mama likes these pages because when she talks about them she moves her fingers around the edges of the pictures. Like she's petting them. It's the same way she moves her fingers along my face after she's through combing my hair.

One of the wraparound pages in the scrapbook has a bunch of pictures of Big Mama and Bettie Jean. "Those pictures were taken when I was 'bout your age," Big Mama says. "My goodness. Look at how young we were!"

Big Mama will lean back on the pillows, holding the book up so she can look at the pictures. She'll have that smile on her face. I call it her rememberies smile.

I lean back on the pillows with her. "Tell me about you and Bettie Jean, Big Mama." I move my fingers over the pictures.

That's when Big Mama will tell about the may'naise sandwiches and sunshine tea.

*B*ettie Jean and I were in the same class. I noticed her all the time because of the pretty clothes she wore. She had sweaters that matched her dresses, and sometimes even shoes that matched her outfits.

She was nice, too. Not like some of the other girls from up her way who acted like they were too good to be friends with just anybody.

Bettie Jean lived uptown. That's where Doctor Hubert One and Doctor Hubert Two lived. The doctor Huberts were brothers—one was a regular doctor and one a dentist.

Bettie Jean's father was the principal of the high school. The one where the black kids went. Her mother was a teacher. They lived in one of the pretty red brick houses on the street where the uptown black folks lived.

My papa did work for a lot of the uptown folks. Like for Mr. Hill, who owned the drugstore, and for the Johnsons, who ran the funeral home. They paid Papa to do things like mow their lawns or weed their gardens or put a fresh coat of paint on the trims of their houses.

Sometimes when Papa had a yard job, he let me go uptown. I liked being with Papa on that pretty street.

One Saturday when I was with Papa, he was working for the Paynes, who lived right next door to Bettie Jean. When Bettie Jean came outside and saw me, she asked if I could come over and play with her in her yard.

Bettie Jean had a big, pretty yard. Papa always said it was one of the prettiest yards in all of uptown, including those on the white folks' uptown street.

At first Bettie Jean and I just ran all over that big yard, playing tag. But then Bettie Jean dragged out a big box of dress-up stuff. There were things in that box that you would not even be able to imagine! Hats with feathers and dresses with long, trailing hems. And shawls—there were all kinds of shawls. Some with fringe, some with beads, some made of velvet and even of silk.

Bettie Jean and I used what we found in that box to become everything we ever dreamed of becoming. Queens. Movie stars. Great artists. Rulers of great lands. Discoverers of miracle cures.

Just about the time I was an empress and Bettie Jean a famous explorer, her mother brought out lunch, a special picnic just for us.

There was a big black-cherry tree in the backyard. Under it was a table, two chairs, and a bench. Everything was made of metal and painted white, but each piece had been carved so that it looked lacy and delicate.

Bettie Jean's mother laid out our lunch on that lacy table. Each of us had a sandwich piled high with tuna fish, lettuce, and tomatoes, and a glass of frosty, sweet lemonade to wash it all down.

It was a perfect lunch for an empress and an explorer. Bettie Jean and I had a perfect time.

The next Saturday Bettie Jean called me on the phone. Her daddy had to do some work at his school, she said. The school was near my house, and Bettie Jean wanted to come along with her daddy so she and I could play in my yard.

Mama said it would be fine. I could hardly wait for Bettie Jean to get there.

My yard wasn't big like Bettie Jean's, but we lived at the edge of a big hill. The hill was covered with soft grass, and there weren't many trees. It was a good hill for running and playing, so that's where I took Bettie Jean.

First we stayed near the bottom of the hill. We played statues. Bettie Jean always froze herself in a monster pose. I always posed like a royal person. Then we would look at each other, bust out laughing, and fall on the soft green grass.

That hill was perfect for rolling. So that's what we did. We rolled and rolled and rolled down the hill. We got big grass stains on our dresses, but we didn't care.

Me and Bettie Jean.

That rolling made us hungry, so I ran in to ask Mama if she would please fix us a special lunch that we could eat outside.

"We don't have anything special for lunch," my mama said.

"Please, Mama," I begged. "Anything, just so we can have a picnic like we did when we played at Bettie Jean's house."

"Okay, Little Miss." That's what my mama called me sometimes. "One special picnic for two coming up," she said.

Mama brought out two little baskets. Each one had a sandwich wrapped in a paper napkin and a glass filled with something cool.

"Here you are," Mama said. "May'naise sandwiches and sunshine tea."

I felt kinda funny. Like not wanting to look at Bettie Jean when Mama handed us the baskets. I wished Mama had fixed us some sandwiches piled high with something, or spread with something pretty, like red jelly.

"I've never had may'naise sandwiches or sunshine tea. What are they?" Bettie Jean asked, all excited, like she was getting something extra special.

"Well," said Mama, "a may'naise sandwich is two pieces of bread with may'naise in between. And sunshine tea—well, if you've never had sunshine tea, you're in for a real treat. Looking through a glass of sunshine tea is being able to watch the sun dance."

"What's in the tea?" Bettie Jean asked. She was already holding the glass up in front of her face.

"Just sugar water," Mama said. "You see, that's the secret of may'naise sandwiches and sunshine tea. There's nothing much in either to keep your mind on what you're eating. So while you're getting full, you can have your mind on other things. Like wondering how the sun can dance."

Mama winked at us and went on back into the house.

Bettie Jean and me ate our lunches and talked about that dancing sun.

That night at supper I told Papa about having Bettie Jean over. I told him about playing statues and rolling down the hill and having may'naise sandwiches and sunshine tea and watching the sun dance.

"Bettie Jean said it was the best lunch she ever had." I was so proud to tell my papa that.

Mama smiled. "I don't think our Little Miss thought Bettie Jean was going to like having may'naise sandwiches for lunch," she said.

Papa looked at me in that way he had. That way of making me want to watch him close and listen real good.

"Nothing shameful 'bout sometimes havin' food that's kinda thin on the fixings, Little Miss. Nothin' shameful at all."

I kept quiet 'cause I knew Papa wasn't through talking.

"The important thing is to use those thin fixings to help you imagine a full-up plate. A plate piled high with everything you want. It's a fact that those thin fixings can make you determined to get a plate that's piled high."

Then my papa touched my cheeks with his fingers and laughed.

Hearing my papa laugh was like seeing the sun dance.

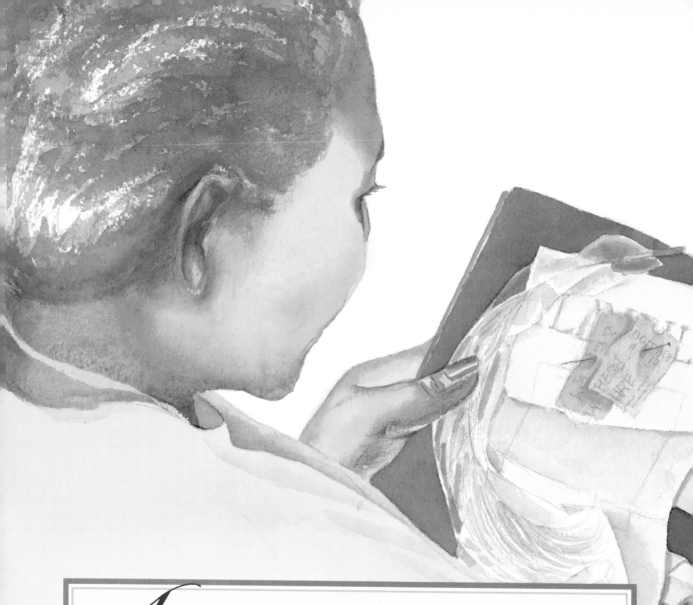

After Big Mama finishes telling me about the may'naise sandwiches and sunshine tea, she asks if I know what Greatgrand Papa meant. When I say I don't really understand everything, she says, "Keep on thinking about it, Little Miss. You'll figure it out."

So I do.

I think about it when Big Mama and I look at some of the other pages in her book.

Like the pictures of Big Mama in her long gown and funny flat hat. "My graduation picture," she says. "When I received my college degree."

Like the ticket stubs pinned next to the picture of Uncle Wilbert. "Wilbert had always dreamed of acting in a grand hall," Big Mama tells me. "And on his opening night, everybody in the family was there. We took up two entire rows!"

I think about it especially when Big Mama and I get ready to go downstairs to the kitchen to fix ourselves a special lunch.

"Let's see," she says as we leave the bed and comfortable pillows. "What's it gonna be today? Should we pile our plates high with some of the good fixings we have? Or maybe—maybe have some may'naise sandwiches and sunshine tea?"

Then Big Mama laughs.

And I can just see that old sun dance.

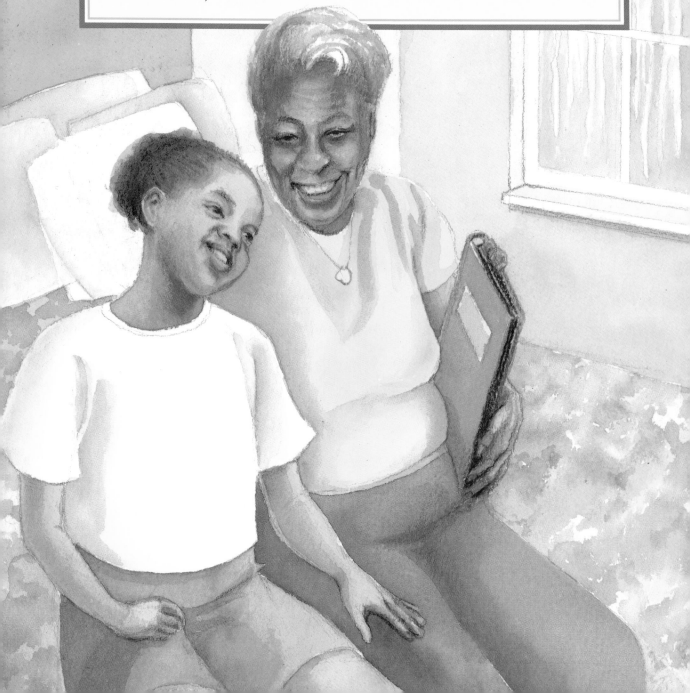